For Will and Justin, again

First edition 2012

Library of Congress Cataloging-in-Publication Data is available.
Library of Congress Catalog Card Number pending
ISBN 978-0-7636-5599-0

12 13 14 15 16 17 CCP 10 9 8 7 6 5 4 3 2 1

Printed in Shenzhen, Guangdong, China

This book was typeset in New Century Schoolbook.
The illustrations were created digitally and in Chinese ink.

Candlewick Press
99 Dover Street
Somerville, Massachusetts 02144

visit us at www.candlewick.com

THIS IS NOT MY HAT

JON KLASSEN

CANDLEWICK PRESS

This hat is not mine.
I just stole it.

I stole it from a big fish.

He was asleep when I did it.

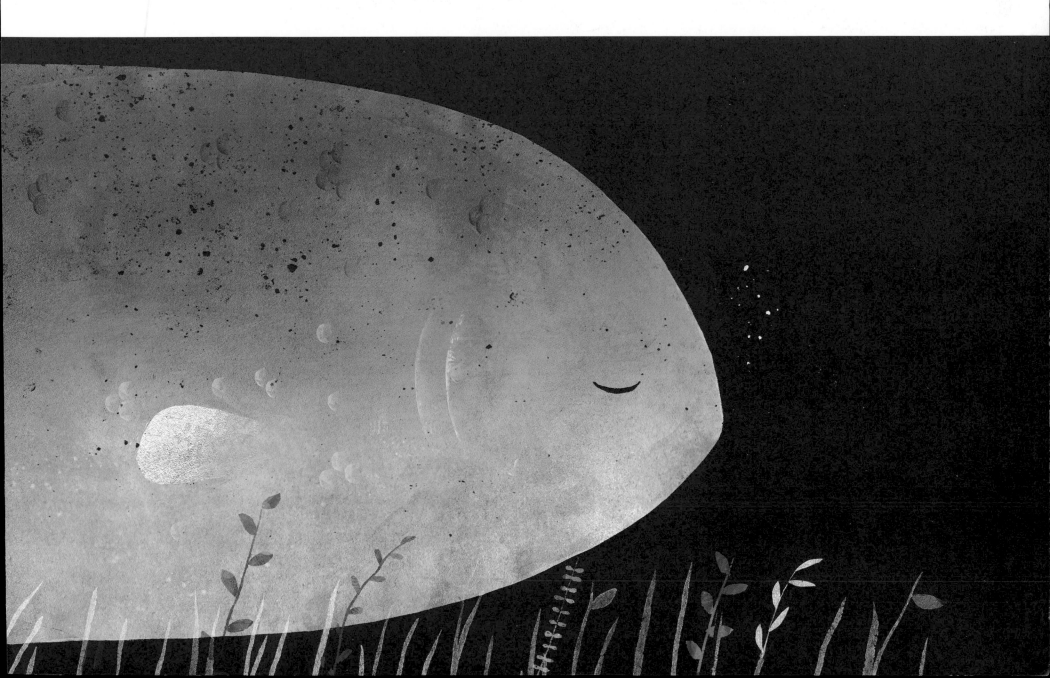

And he probably won't wake up for a long time.

And even if he does wake up,

he probably won't notice that it's gone.

And even if he does notice that it's gone,

he probably won't know it was me who took it.

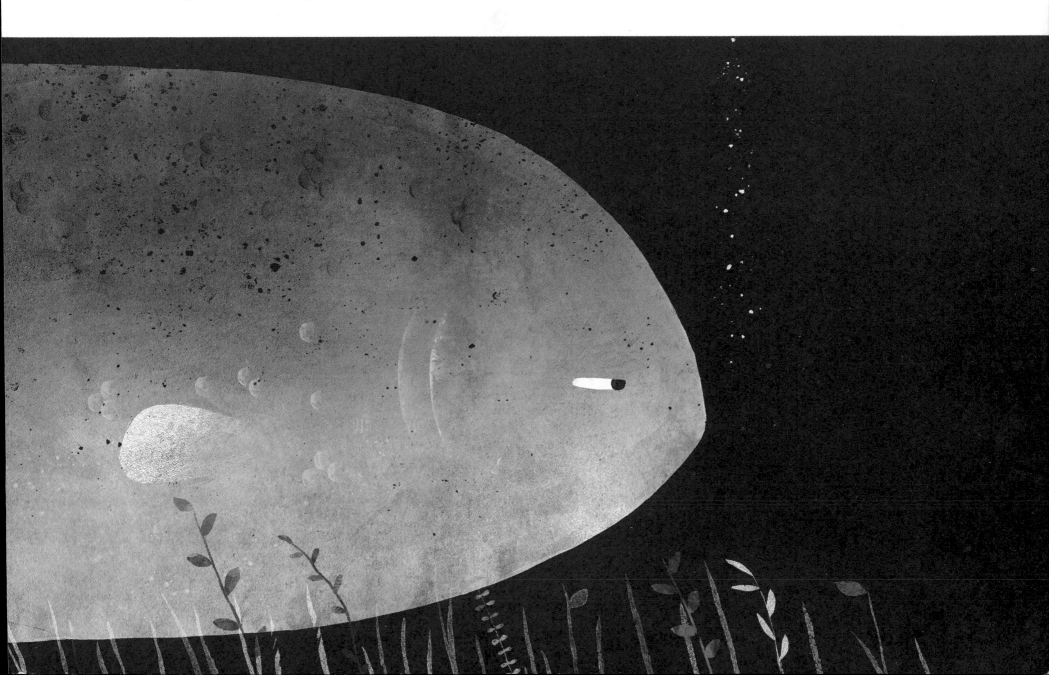

And even if he does guess it was me,

he won't know where I am going.

But I will tell you where I am going.
I am going where the plants grow
big and tall and close together.

It is very hard to see in there.
Nobody will ever find me.

There is someone who saw me already.
But he said he wouldn't tell anyone
which way I went.

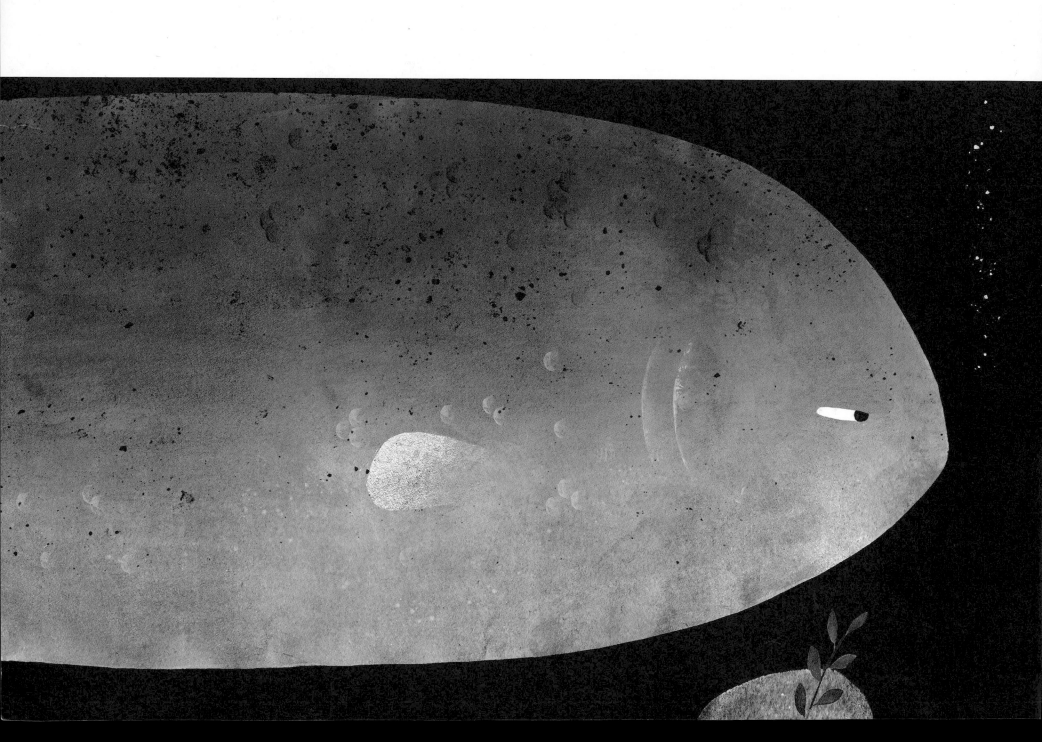

So I am not worried about that.

I know it's wrong to steal a hat.
I know it does not belong to me.
But I am going to keep it.
It was too small for him anyway.
It fits me just right.

And look! I made it!

Where the plants are big and tall and close together!

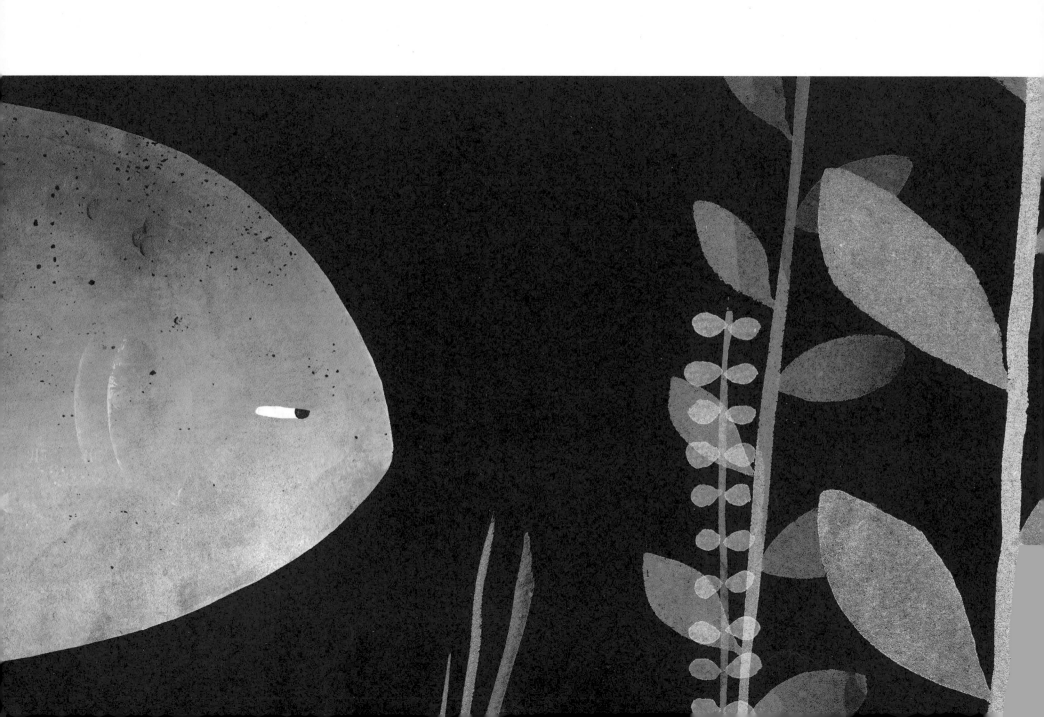

I knew I was going to make it.

Nobody will ever find me.